To

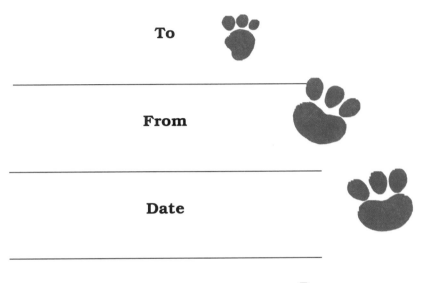

_____

From

_____

Date

_____

Animal Kingdom

Animal Kingdom

Stories by Joanne E. De Jonge

Illustrations by Samuel J. Butcher

Baker Books

A Division of Baker Book House Co
Grand Rapids, Michigan 49516

Library of Congress Cataloging-in-Publication Data

De Jonge, Joanne E., 1943–
   Animal kingdom / stories by Joanne E. De Jonge ; illustrations by
Samuel J. Butcher.
      p. cm.
   Summary: A collection of stories about animals, including a bear,
elephant, and whale.
   ISBN 0-8010-4264-X (cloth)
   1. Animals—Juvenile fiction. 2. Children's stories, American. [1.
Animals—Fiction. 2. Short stories.] I. Butcher, Samuel J. (Samuel
John), 1939– ill. II. Title. III. Title: Precious moments
PZ7.D3678An 1996
[E]—dc20
                                                          96-27807

Contents

Letter to Parents

These stories will open the world of nature to you and your children and incidentally can open pathways of discussion between child and adult. Told simply enough for a child to understand, often the stories also contain concepts adults will appreciate. The antics of the animals will encourage talk about love, generosity, self-image, cultural differences, and other important issues. The stories do not preach, only gently imply or suggest.

Although they are whimsical, the stories accurately portray animal habitats and behaviors. The difference between fiction and fact will be obvious. Of course, bees, frogs, and bears don't talk human language. But did you know that some bees live in the ground, only male frogs sing, and bears always defer to skunks?

So, read and enjoy! Revel in Tubby Piglet's mud puddle. Listen to Freddy Frog's strange song. Chuckle at Ollie Boom-Boom.

Then take some time to talk about the stories with your children. Because, like most good things, these stories are best when they are shared.

Joanne E. De Jonge

Good Neighbors

Blossom was a good bear at heart. But it was easy to forget about his good heart because he thought only about himself and didn't remember to be kind to others.

If something moved into his path, he chased it away without looking twice. If he found a bush with lots of berries, he ate the whole thing. When he ignored other woodland creatures, he thought nothing of it.

He didn't have time for others, he told himself. He was too busy gathering grubs and berries. Woodland meetings and parties were a waste of his time.

That's why he missed the party for Buzzy. The new little bee had arrived, all alone, to make his home in the woodlot. As was their custom, older woodlot creatures had a welcoming party for Buzzy. But Blossom did not even think about welcoming the lonely little bee.

The very next morning Blossom rumbled out of his den looking for some breakfast food. He found a bush, almost covered with berries, licked his lips, and sat down to the feast.

"Hey, you're sitting on top of my door!" piped a small voice underneath him. "Please move, Blossom."

Blossom didn't hear a thing. He never listened to other creatures.

"I don't want to do this . . ." the voice warned. "I'm sorry, but here goes!"

"YEOW!!!" Blossom howled. He jumped up and rubbed his bottom. "That hurt! What was it?"

"That was me," Buzzy piped in his ear. "I warned you. You sat right on my front

door. I couldn't get out, and I couldn't get any air."

"But you're a bee," Blossom said. "Bees live in hives. Why were you in the ground?"

"If you had been at the party you would have known," Buzzy explained.

"Many bees live in holes in the ground, just like I do. The ants warned me about you, Blossom. They said that you sit on them all the time."

"Oh," Blossom said softly. "You mean I've sat on ants and didn't know it? I'm so sorry. I didn't know I was hurting them."

"I know," Buzzy answered. "But you really should think about your neighbors and do some kind things for them once in a while. I know you have a good heart and you should listen to what it tells you to

do. You don't want to get stung again, do you?"

"NO!" Blossom said quickly. Then he sat quietly for a long time. Finally he said, "I want to be a good neighbor. I'll try very hard to listen to my good heart and get to know the other creatures."

Now Blossom goes to the woodland meetings and parties and is becoming a friendly neighbor. And he always looks before he sits down in the woods.

A Beaver's Tale

Benji never liked his tail. When he was a tiny beaver in his family's lodge, he complained about it.

"Is that my tail?" he asked when he first saw it. "Do all beavers have such horrible tails?"

"Shhh," his mother had whispered softly. "You have a perfectly good beaver tail. Don't complain." And she gently combed his fur.

When Benji grew up and began to explore, he complained even more.

"Ricky Raccoon has a cool striped tail," he whined. "Why can't beavers have striped tails? I wish I had a soft, round, furry tail. What good is this big paddle? I look like a fish."

"You look like a beaver," his mother said gently. "Some day you'll appreciate your tail. Just be glad you've got it."

"I'm not glad," Benji whined again. "I hate my tail."

Day and night Benji complained. Then he pouted, then he complained again. But, of course, he couldn't change his tail.

Early one morning Father shook him awake. "Benji, come quickly," he ordered. "We've had a heavy rain. The pond is flooding and the lodge may break. We need everybody's help."

All the beavers streamed out of the lodge and got to work. Older family members went across the pond to cut big trees. Young Benji was put on watch duty.

"You may cut a few saplings," Mother said, "but stay alert. Crafty Coyote would love to snatch one of us or tear up our lodge. Let us know if you see him coming."

Benji cut a few saplings as he watched for the coyote. But soon Benji grew tired of his job. He forgot to watch carefully.

That's why he didn't see the crafty coyote quietly come to the edge of the pond. He was very close when Benji saw him.

20

What can I do? Benji wondered desperately. *If I say anything, the coyote will see the lodge. If I don't, he'll see my family.*

Suddenly Benji knew what to do. He swam behind the lodge, turned around, and with all his might, slapped his tail hard on the water. The S-L-A-P echoed over the pond and through the woods. Crafty Coyote jumped when he heard the SLAP. He was confused and looked around. Benji's family saw the danger and hurried back underwater to their home.

Inside their lodge, Benji's whole family gathered around him. "Thank you, Benji; you saved us!" They mewed in pleasure.

"Good job, Benji," his parents said. "Crafty Coyote has no idea where we are."

21

Mother added quietly, "I wonder if you could have done that with a soft, round, furry tail."

The Business of Bees

"YEEOW!" screamed Teddy Bear. "Why did the Creator make bees? Are they here to sting us?"

"When you take only your share, you'll know the real reason," answered Blossom Bear. "Honeybees are here to give us honey."

"I thought they were here to give us flowers," whispered a butterfly. "Without bees as partners, many flowers would never make seeds. Where would we go for sweet juice next year?"

"Honeybees are here," added Dancie the

Deer, "to give us apples and other fruits. Everyone knows that without bees, flowers on fruit trees would never become fruits. What would we eat?"

"I always thought," piped up Wiggles the Caterpillar, "that bees are here to make music in the meadows. I would miss their merry buzzes if honeybees didn't come to my meadow in the spring."

"Nonsense," croaked Freddy Frog. "The bees are all here to add cheerful colors. If honeybees disappeared, wouldn't you miss those bright fuzzy stripes?"

Some birds even added their reasons. "Bees are good food," they chirped. "But only after they've finished their life," they added quickly.

All the creatures were glad the Creator had made honeybees, even though they

couldn't agree
on exactly why
he made them.

The Sweetest Carrot

Four bunny brothers—Hippity, Hop, Flippity, and Flop—often ate together at the edge of the woodlot. Mother Rabbit

27

always took them to the best places. There was plenty of sweet grass for all but they often quarreled just a bit.

"This is my grass," Hippity often scolded Hop. "You find your own."

"Why does Flippity always get the sweetest plants?" Flop usually whined.

"Shhh," Mother would say. "There's plenty for all. The best way to enjoy a good thing is to share it." But the bunny brothers didn't understand.

Early one morning as they crept to the side of the woods near their home, Flop noticed something strange under a bush in the meadow. He gathered all his courage and hopped over for a look. There he found a huge, juicy carrot!

"Look what I found!" he grinned as he showed his brothers.

"I get some!" "Give me a bite!" "No fair!" "I saw it first!" "It's mine!" All the bunnies talked through each other.

Then Flop, who was the oldest brother and a little weary of quarrels, said loudly, "I found it and I'm tired of selfish arguments. I'm going to give it away." And he hopped over to Missy, their lonely neighbor.

"Mom, stop him!" cried Flippity.

"Now I won't get any!" wailed Hop.

But Mother just said, "Shhh," and watched.

"This is for you," Flop told Missy as he handed her the carrot.

"Thank you, Flop!" Missy was delighted. "I can't possibly eat the whole thing. I'm alone, you know. Maybe your brothers would like some." Together, they took the carrot back to the family.

"Well, look at that," **Hippity** whispered. "Flop didn't lose a **carrot. He** gained a friend." Hippity took **a big** bite. But he was careful to leave **plenty for** the others.

They all shared that **carrot. And** never before had any carrot **tasted so sweet.**

Butterfly-to-Be

Wiggles never thought of himself as a caterpillar. He always thought he was a butterfly-to-be. He could hardly wait to grow up.

"When I grow up, I'll have such beautiful wings," he often told himself. "I'll drink sweet juices from flowers, and I'll fly off to faraway fields."

Butterflies who heard Wiggles often said, "Don't be in such a hurry. Don't wish your life away."

One very wise butterfly said, "You'll become a butterfly when you are older. Meanwhile, you're a very fine caterpillar."

"I don't want to be a caterpillar," Wiggles complained. "I want to be a butterfly now." But the Creator didn't want him to become a butterfly just yet.

One day, as Wiggles sat on a bush waiting to grow up, a little girl noticed him. "What a cute fuzzy caterpillar," she said as she picked him up. "Look at all those

legs! I wonder why he's got all these stripes."

"He is cute," a deep voice agreed. "That's a woolly bear caterpillar. Lots of people look for woolly bears every fall. They think they can tell if the winter will be cold by looking at this caterpillar's stripes. Of course they can't, but we'd better put this one back where you found him. Other people will want to see him."

Wiggles felt himself placed on the grass near his favorite bush. He lay very still for a long time. He thought and thought and thought.

"Now do you get it?" the wise butterfly whispered nearby. "You are very special!"

"I am?" Wiggles couldn't believe his ears. "I am a special caterpillar!" He crawled back to his bush and ate and ate and ate.

Wiggles never again wished to be a butterfly. He was perfectly happy as a caterpillar.

Of course, he did become a butterfly—at exactly the right time. And now Wiggles looks for unhappy little caterpillars. "Just wait," he tells them, "you will change when you get older. Meanwhile, you're fine just the way you are."

The Camel's Heart

Long, long ago a camel met a lost monkey
in the middle of a desert. The monkey was

36

very hot and thirsty and had a very bad tummyache. He felt so sick.

"Let me take you home," offered the kind camel. "I have feet made to run in the sand. I have three sets of eyelids and two sets of eyelashes to keep sand out of my eyes. And I have lots of hair in my ears and my nose to keep them clean. And I can go for days without water."

The camel was not bragging. She was just stating the facts and wanted the monkey to know that she would take good care of him. The monkey was too sick to listen closely and did not understand that the camel was being kind and would take him home quickly.

"That camel is so proud," the little monkey said when he was safely home. "You should hear her brag about herself."

The kind camel said nothing. But the monkey's words hurt her heart.

Never again will I open my heart to another monkey, she thought.

From that day on the camel stayed away from monkeys. When a monkey came close, she grunted and grumbled and spit.

Under a camel's cranky bluffing is a tender heart. Only a few monkeys know that. Now the kind camel has other animal friends, and they have many happy talks on long, dusty walks in the desert.

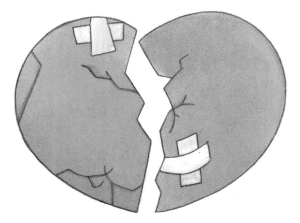

Why Cheetahs Are So Swift

Mama Cheetah and her son sat patiently waiting to enter the big ark boat.

"Take a good look at the great outdoors," Mama said quietly. "We'll be in that ark for a long, long time." So they both sat and looked and looked at the world around them.

"What are you doing way out here?" a raven scolded. "Almost everyone's in the ark. If you're still here when that door closes . . ."

"Oh dear," Mama cried as she turned around. "We weren't watching closely. Run as fast as you can, son." And the cheetahs ran as fast as they could.

But the little cheetah soon became tired. He slowed to a walk. Mama stayed at his side. She almost gave up hope of reaching the ark in time. "Please help us," she cried.

Suddenly a strong wind blew up behind the cheetahs. It roared into their muscles

and bones. Both cheetahs ran as fast as the wind—faster than any animal had ever run—straight to the ark.

"Thank you," Mama whispered to the Creator as he shut the door with the cheetahs inside.

And that's why cheetahs are the fastest four-footed creatures on earth.

41

The Donkey and Her Master

Long ago there lived a donkey named
Beeor. Her home was near a small town
in a faraway country. She lived with a few

chickens—who never talked—and her master—who talked a lot.

Beeor loved her master. She gladly carried him into town, and sometimes on long journeys. But her master thought that Beeor was not a very smart donkey. The master never dreamed that a donkey could have thoughts and feelings. So he wasn't especially kind to Beeor.

One morning Beeor's master saddled her up for a long journey. Neither of them knew that this journey would go down in history.

As they began their journey, her master guided her down a path through a field. Suddenly, Beeor saw an angel standing in the middle of the path. He held up a sword as if to say, "Stop!"

Beeor stopped. But her master kicked her and yelled, "Get going!" So she walked around the angel into the field.

Her master was angry, so angry he was shaking. He used a stick he always car-

ried to hit Beeor on the rump. "Get back on the path, you foolish donkey," he yelled.

Then the path became very narrow. Stone walls lined either side. As Beeor plodded between the walls the angel appeared again. This time he raised a hand as if to say, "Go no farther."

Beeor slowed down and stopped, but felt a sharp *thwump* on her rump again. So she squeezed very close to one wall to get around the angel. Beeor squeezed so close that she scraped her back end. She also crushed her master's foot against the wall.

"Crazy, stubborn donkey," her master yelled. He beat her very hard. "What's the matter with you?"

Then the angel flew to a really narrow spot in the path and stood with both

hands raised. This time Beeor could not squeeze past. Nor could she turn around. So she did the only thing she could; she lay down.

46

Now her master was so angry. He yelled and lost his temper and beat Beeor harder than he had ever beat her before. "Get up! Go, you stubborn beast," he yelled. The angel didn't move. The path was blocked.

Beeor could take no more. Her master treated her like she had no feelings. She must talk. "What have I done to you to make you beat me these three times?" Beeor asked.

Her master blinked in surprise. "You have made me so angry!" he answered. "If I had a sword in my hand, I would kill you right now."

"Am I not your own donkey, which you have always ridden to this day?" Beeor reasoned with him. "Have I been in the habit of doing this to you?"

"No," he answered.

The angel held up his sword again, and Beeor feared for their lives.

Then God opened her master's eyes so that he could see the angel. Immediately,

48

the master fell flat on his face in front of the angel.

Beeor's master and the angel had a little talk. Beeor didn't hear the whole thing. But she did hear the angel say, "The donkey saw me . . . If she had not turned away, I would certainly have killed you by now, but I would have spared her."

Then the angel stepped aside and let them go on. But Beeor noticed that the angel followed them. Nothing happened on the rest of the journey.

We all know that animals don't talk. Talking animal stories are fun to read, but not true. This talking animal story is true. You can read it in Numbers 22, in the Bible.

Why Me?

Elsa Elephant cried for a whole year after she was brought to the circus. She was lonely and sad and missed her African family.

50

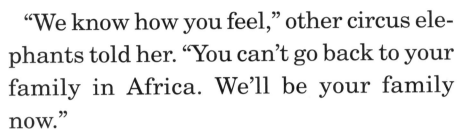

"We know how you feel," other circus elephants told her. "You can't go back to your family in Africa. We'll be your family now."

But Elsa didn't want a new family. She wanted her African family. "Why me?" she always cried. "What did I do to deserve this?"

"You did nothing," one wise elephant told her. "Life isn't always fair. Make the best of it."

But Elsa couldn't. "Why me?" she cried again. And the more she thought about how sad she was, the sadder she became.

Then Elsa met a tiny creature, a mouse. One look at the unhappy little mouse told Elsa that he was in trouble.

"Which way to the woodland?" he gasped at Elsa.

"I should know?" she whined. "I've been stuck in the circus for a year. Who are you? What's wrong with you?"

"I'm Dewey and I'm lost," the mouse whispered weakly. "Please help me." And then he fainted.

Elsa quickly sucked water from a nearby tank and sprayed Dewey.

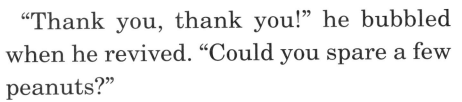

"Thank you, thank you!" he bubbled when he revived. "Could you spare a few peanuts?"

"Doesn't someone feed you?" Elsa wondered aloud.

"I find my own food at home," Dewey piped, "but I don't know how to find it here."

"Poor Dewey," Elsa sighed as she set a few peanuts at his side. "I've got plenty. They keep me well supplied."

So Elsa helped Dewey become healthy and strong. Then she found a circus mouse who knew the way to the woodland. She sent him on his way with a few more peanuts.

Elsa forgot her own problems for a full week. She had helped Dewey instead. And she had never been happier.

Elsa still misses her family. But she's too busy to say, "Why me?" She's helping others who have troubles.

Elsa can't remember the last time she cried, even though elephants have very good memories.

Freddy's Song

Freddy Frog sat alone on a lily pad, lost in thought. Zap! He flicked out his tongue to catch a tasty bug.

"Hey, let me go!" yelled Buzzy Bee. "Don't you know I can sting?"

"Sorry, Buzzy," Freddy croaked. "I wasn't paying attention. I was thinking about finding myself a wife. All the creatures are starting families, and I'm still all alone."

"Have you joined the male chorus?" Buzzy asked. "That's the way the other frogs find wives. Their songs keep me up all night."

"But I'm different," Freddy sighed. "I just know I'm different. Do you think it will work anyway?"

"Doesn't hurt to try," Buzzy answered as he buzzed away.

That night Freddy joined the male chorus. Immediately, he knew he was different. Most of the frogs sang, "Ribet! Ribet!"

A few sang, "Rabat! Rabat!" But when Freddy opened his mouth, he croaked, "Kneedeep! Kneedeep!" He was so embarrassed. He left quickly.

"I'm so different, no one wants me," he sighed. "I'll be lonely the rest of my life." And he hopped up onto a toadstool—he called it a frogstool—to think lonely thoughts.

But he wasn't alone for long. Pokey, the wise old turtle, had been looking for him. "I heard your song last night," Pokey said softly, "and I thought it was wonderful."

"What good is that?" Freddy asked. "You're a turtle. I need another frog just like me."

"Your song was wonderful," Pokey went on patiently, "because I haven't heard it for many years.

"You are different, Freddy. You are very special. Years ago there were many frogs just like you. But most of them disappeared. No one knows why. You're one of a very few.

"Don't give up on your song. If there's another frog just like you around, she'll hear it. Besides, I think it's one of the most beautiful frog songs I've heard."

That night, before Freddy joined the male chorus he told himself, "I'm different; I'm special. I'm special. I'm very special."

All the frogs sang "Ribet!" or "Rabat!" Freddy listened for a few minutes and then he sang "KNEEDEEP" just as loudly as he could. When the lady frogs came to pick their favorite singers, Freddy kept singing. When almost all the other frogs had gone to their homes, Freddy was still singing.

He was about to give up at dawn. Suddenly he saw something move near his feet. Up hopped Freeda, the most beautiful frog Freddy had ever seen. She was just like him!

"I've listened many nights for that song,"

she sighed. "I thought I'd never hear it. Why did you wait so long to sing it?"

Freddy went home with Freeda. They had lots of little tadpoles that summer. All the boys sing just like Freddy. And none of them are embarrassed by that. They know they are very special frogs.

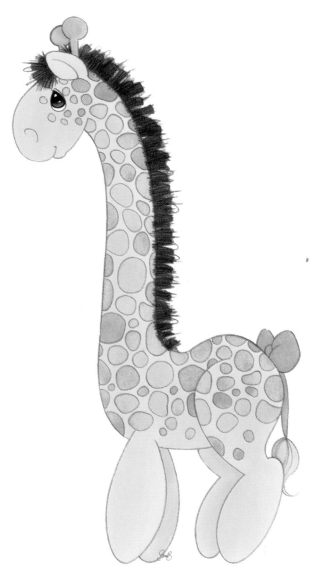

If Only . . .

If only I had short front legs, the little giraffe thought, *I could drink much more easily.* His Creator, who knew better than

the little giraffe, heard the wish. Immediately the little giraffe had short front legs.

The next time the grassland creatures ran from the lions, the little giraffe fell behind. Just in time, his Creator gave him long front legs again.

If only I didn't have such a long neck, the little giraffe thought, *I could eat grass just like the zebras.*

His Creator, who knew better than the little giraffe, heard the wish. Immediately, the little giraffe had a short neck.

But the zebras ate the best grass. Little giraffe looked with longing at the tender leaves atop the trees. He grew very, very hungry. Just in time, his Creator gave him a long neck again.

Little giraffe ate his leaves gratefully. And he ran like the wind. And he was

very thankful for a while. But soon he forgot.

He looked with envy at the zebras' stripes. *If only* . . . he began. But then he remembered how the lions almost caught him and how he almost starved. He did not finish his sentence.

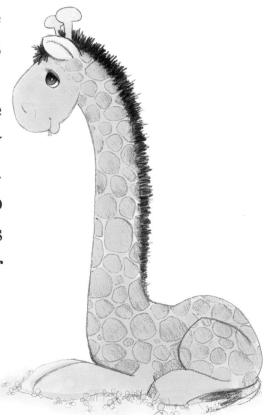

The little giraffe still doesn't know why he has spots. But he's going to live with his spots because his Creator knows best.

To Each His Own

"He's much too bold if you ask me," the chickens said.

"Bold is OK," the horse put in. "But he eats anything."

"I don't mind what he eats," added the lamb. "But that beard looks awful."

Each barnyard animal said something almost unkind about the new goat. They had never before seen a goat. "There's one thing wrong with that youngster," the cow

65

finished the discussion. "He's far too frisky."

None of that bothered Billy the Goat. He was waiting for something more important.

Soon another goat arrived at the farm. And all the animals were saying unkind things again. This time, Billy butted into their talk. "She's a perfectly good goat. She's not timid, and I like her appetite. I think her beard is beautiful."

"To each his own," the chickens clucked. But then they added, "The goats are brave and do help us when we're scared."

"They're not so bad," the horse agreed. "And we won't fight over food."

"Beards are OK for goats," the lamb said. "After all, everybody's different."

"That's right," they all agreed. "Everybody's different. To each his own." And they all got along splendidly.

The Hippo's Diet

"Anybody can see that you're much too fat," the monkey told the hippo.

"You really think so?" she asked. "This

is the way I've been made. And I eat only salads. What do you suppose I should do?"

"Go on a diet." The monkey sounded very wise. "Eat less."

The hippo tried. She ate very few water weeds and nothing more.

69

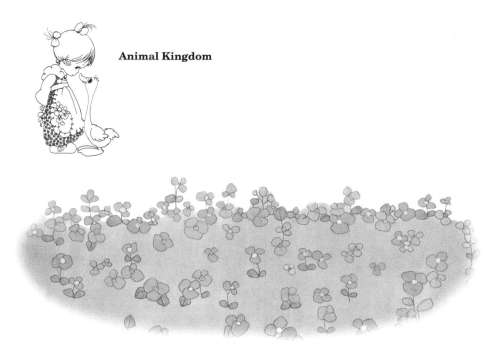

The water weeds she ignored grew wildly. They choked rivers and crept into ponds. Animals who came to drink or swim found more weeds than water.

And the hippo became weak with hunger. She couldn't move. Grass grew over all her trails. No other animal could beat it down as well as she had. Travel on trails ground to a halt.

"Anybody can see that you're much too thin," her neighbors told her.

"I think so too," she said happily. "I was made big and fat for a reason. Let me at those salads."

70

The hippo ate and grew fat once more.
All animals drank, and swam, and trav-
eled freely again. The hippo never again
went on a diet. And even the monkey did
not call her fat.

Monkey Business

Many years ago, the Big Cat Family held a reunion in the local jungle. All the

cousins—leopards, tigers, lions, cheetahs, bobcats, and so forth—came.

The whole jungle was filled with excitement when the big cats came into the clearing. Never before had jungle creatures seen such wonderful cats! Each seemed more beautiful than the others.

Except Leo, the only lion who came from a distant land. The jungle creatures thought his tan coat and his shaggy mane made him look so plain and ragged.

"I don't know him," said a monkey. "But I think his coat is awful."

Then the monkeys had a wonderful idea. "Let's give him a new coat!" they chattered. "We can make him look a lot better."

So they found some paint, brushes, and

scissors. The next time Leo took a nap, they set to work.

First, they cut off his shaggy mane. Then they worked on his coat. One started in front, another in back. When

they met in the middle they saw their mistake. One had painted spots, the other had painted stripes. "Oophs! Oh, well," they said. "We'll call him a liger or a tion. There's no difference."   ”

All the creatures were very proud of themselves. After the Big Cats went home, the monkeys often told the story of how they gave plain Leo a colorful new coat and a haircut.

Many years later the Big Cats planned another reunion. Before they arrived, the local leopard called the monkeys together. "My dear friends," he began. "I know you are very kind and helpful. But this time, please don't paint the lion; and, never touch his mane."

The jungle creatures looked at each other in confusion.

"Spots are great for me," the leopard explained. They look like patches of sunlight in the jungle. Stripes work well for tigers but lions live in open spaces. Spots and stripes are so easy to see. Every

grassland creature saw Leo coming for miles. And they laughed at his very short mane.

"Some of my relatives are different from me. But different is not better or worse. It's just different."

When Leo arrived, all the monkeys apologized, one by one. Leo laughed and said, "That's OK. You just didn't know me, so you thought I looked strange. I know you'll remember now that different is neither better nor worse—just different."

Dewey Finds His Place

Dewey Mouse had a wonderful idea. He would leave the woodland for the winter. Instead of scurrying under snow and

scratching frozen ground for food, he'd relax in Farmer Jones's warm house. "I'll return next spring," he promised.

"You'll never return," his relatives warned him. "Any mouse who tried that has disappeared forever. Don't go. We need a good strong mouse like you."

"Please stay," his friends begged. But Dewey did not change his mind.

"You belong in the woodlot," drawled Pokey Turtle, who was very old and very wise. "But, if you must go, I'll take you.

78

I've been there." So Dewey packed his bags, scrambled atop Pokey, and said good-by to his friends and relatives.

He thoroughly enjoyed his first two nights in the big house. It was cozy, and there was plenty to eat. Of course, mice will eat almost anything.

The third night he discovered a sugar bowl. He had never tasted sugar before. It was so good that he snacked all night. At dawn, he fell asleep right in the sugar bowl. That's where they found him.

"EEEK, A MOUSE!!" Dewey recognized a human voice. He scampered out of the bowl, streaked off the table, slipped under the sink, and squeezed through a crack in a wall before he stopped.

He could hear people move everything under the sink, looking for him. So he sat just as quietly as he could.

"It's just a mouse," a voice said. "But it doesn't belong here."

80

"Throw out the sugar," Mrs. Jones wailed. "It's full of germs."

"I'll set the traps," Farmer Jones promised.

"Oh, oh," Dewey gasped. "Pokey told me that traps are trouble—big trouble. No wonder some mice have never returned home. I must be very, very careful."

And he was. He never stayed in the kitchen. He left no signs that he had been there. He slept inside the wall by day. If he sneaked a midday snack, he walked on tiptoes. And he never, never touched the trap under the sink.

One night Dewey carefully slipped through the crack under the sink. He looked around cautiously and sniffed the air. A new smell was in the kitchen. It wasn't food. It was—sniff, sniff, sniff! CAT!! Dewey knew about cats. All the woodland creatures could tell stories of

close calls with stray pets. But it took Dewey too long to recognize cat smell.

The cat had darted between Dewey and the wall, cutting off Dewey's retreat. Dewey scrambled up the cupboard look-

ing for a safe place. He tore across the counter, jumped into a lunch box, and pulled the top closed just in time. "I want to go home," he cried. Then he fell asleep, exhausted.

He slept right through all the jiggles and bumps as the farmer's daughter took her lunch to school. The next thing he knew, he saw light above his head. She had opened her lunch box. But only for a second.

EEK, there's the mouse, she thought. And she closed the box very quickly. But she was a very brave little girl. She didn't scream or cry. She put her lunch box away and said nothing. Dewey waited nervously inside.

That afternoon the box juggled and bumped back home. Suddenly, it opened, then shook, and Dewey tumbled out. He

landed right in Farmer Jones's pumpkin
patch.

"Run away, little mouse," said the little
girl. "You belong in the woods, not in the

house." So Dewey disappeared beneath the nearest leaf.

"I've been waiting for you," a nearby voice whispered. It was good old Pokey. "I hoped you would make it out of there. Climb aboard." And Pokey took Dewey home.

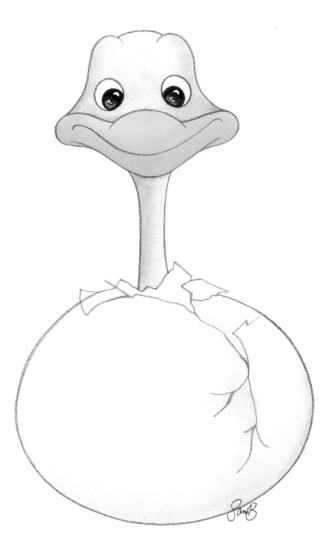

Ollie Boom-Boom

Ollie hatched with a smile on his face.

"I'm Ollie," he boomed. "Glad to meet you."

His neighbors stepped back in surprise. "He hatched from an egg and he has wings," they whispered to each other. "He must be a bird. But birds cheep, they don't boom."

"What are you?" they asked Ollie.

"I'm Ollie," he boomed again. "Glad to meet you."

So they named him Ollie Boom-Boom. And they tried to figure out exactly what he was.

They looked at his long neck and his two long legs. "Are you some kind of giraffe?" they asked.

"I'm Ollie," he boomed. "I can run very fast and see very far."

They looked at his huge toenails. A bird would have had claws there. "Are you some kind of elephant?" they asked.

"I'm Ollie," he boomed. "Toenails suit me fine when I run."

They looked at his long eyelashes. "Are you some kind of camel?" they asked.

"I'm Ollie," he boomed. "Eyelashes keep dust from my eyes."

One day another creature just like Ollie showed up. "What are you? What are you?" the animals asked.

"Silly creatures," she said. "Why do you need to have a name for everybody? If you must know, I'm an ostrich."

"Ollie, Ollie Boom-Boom," the neighbors called. "You're an ostrich!"

But Ollie didn't really care. He was just happy being who he was.

90

The Song Heard Round the World

Every morning just before the sun rises, owls go to bed with a final song. People say, "The owls are hooting."

But the Creator hears a song of praise. "Thank you for eyes that see in the dark. Thank you for silent wings. Thank you for rest during the day."

Every morning just as the sun rises, bluebirds wake up and sing. People say, "The birds are singing."

But the Creator hears a song of praise. "Thank you for keeping us safe through the night. Thank you for beautiful feathers. Thank you for another gorgeous day."

As the sun moves westward, western owls go to bed with a final song. Western bluebirds wake up with a song. And the Creator hears the song of praise move westward across the world.

Always, somewhere in the world, it is morning. Somewhere people are saying, "The owls are hooting. The birds are singing."

And always, from somewhere in the world, the Creator hears a song of praise.

The Secret of the Mud Puddle

Of all farm animals, pigs have always talked the most. Farmer Jones's animals were used to noisy pigs. That's why they

wondered why the pigs never said a word about mud puddles.

"Why do you lay down in that filthy stuff?" a lamb once asked. The pigs snuggled closer together. But they said nothing.

"Mud bothers me," said a cow. "Why do you love it so?" The pigs ate some more food. But they said nothing.

One day a skunk met Tubby Piglet alone at the edge of the farm. "Your secret is safe with me," she whispered. "Why do you love mud puddles?"

"You've probably noticed," Tubby began, "that we have lots of biting bugs. They drive us crazy. Cows and horses use their tails as fly swatters. Sheep and goats wear woolly coats to protect their skin. We have neither swatters nor coats, so we use mud. That smothers the bugs and soothes our skin."

"That's a good reason," the skunk answered. "Why keep that a secret?"

Tubby lowered his voice to a whisper. "That mud just plain feels good. With or

without biting bugs, we like to lie in mud puddles. Suppose all animals knew how wonderful mud puddles feel. They would all want to roll in the mud. That would

never do. If we don't tell them, they'll never try it."

"Makes sense to me," the skunk answered. And she disappeared into the woodland.

Farm animals still wonder. Pigs aren't about to tell them. But a few children know the secret of the mud puddle.

Dorsey's Reflection

Little Dorsey Porcupine was a gentle, but messy, creature who always kept her quills pointed out in every direction. She

loved her neighbors and wanted to be friends. But they all stayed away from her.

Dorsey tried to make friends. She often threw down choice hemlock bits to nearby deer. They always ran away. She squealed in delight at the sight of another porcupine, but he waddled away as fast as he could. So Dorsey was always alone.

One day, as she plodded through the woods, she found a quiet pond. She trotted to the water's edge for a drink. A fierce-looking creature peered out of the water at her. She was terrified and ran up the nearest tree.

It took her a long time to realize that she had seen her own reflection. *Oh, my!* she said to herself. *That's how all the creatures see me. They're scared of me.*

So she stayed right up in that tree until she had smoothed down all her quills. Then she crept back to the water and peeked in. A friendly little porcupine looked back at her.

Soon Dorsey's neighbors stopped staying away from her. Now she has some very good friends. Deer thank her for hemlock bits. Other porcupines visit her. And everybody knows that she is a very gentle creature.

The first thing each morning Dorsey trundles down to the pool to check her reflection. She wants to make sure she sees herself exactly as others see her.

It's a Gift

Ricky Raccoon was clever. Raccoons usually are clever. Ricky was extra clever. He was almost the smartest raccoon who ever lived.

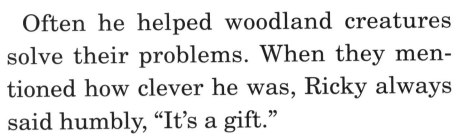

Often he helped woodland creatures solve their problems. When they mentioned how clever he was, Ricky always said humbly, "It's a gift."

But sometimes Ricky looked down on creatures who weren't as clever as he. His gift, he thought, was better than any of their gifts.

Then Pokey, the wise old turtle, would remind him, "God gave us each a gift. Mine's a shell; Lilac's is her smell. Dorsey Porcupine is friendly, and you're smart. Every creature should admire the other's gift."

"You're right," Ricky always agreed. But it was very hard for Ricky to remember that.

That's why Ricky thought proud thoughts as he went fishing one night. *No one fishes this well,* he told himself,

because no one is as clever as I am. Only I know how to turn over these stones to pick up crayfish . . . YEOW! What's that? He pulled up his paw to find a clam attached.

"I thought you were just a flat stone," he whined at the clam. "Why do you look just like a stone?"

"It's a gift," the clam said softly.

Now when Ricky thinks proud thoughts, his paw aches a bit to help Ricky remember that all creatures have gifts.

Good Friends

Chip and Rudy were very good friends.
Chip chatted constantly as he rode on
Rudy's back and happily picked at ticks

tucked into his friend's wrinkled skin. Often he chirped warnings about dangers nearsighted Rudy couldn't see.

Rudy scared away any creature that bothered Chip. Often Rudy kicked up extra tidbits for the bird to eat.

Both friends helped each other. That's what friends do, and they were best of friends until one day Rudy began to think grumpy little thoughts. He never knew why he thought those grumpy things. Maybe he was tired, or having a bad day. Anyway, the grumpy thoughts came.

Chip chatters so, Rudy thought. *And he's always pecking my hide. There's no peace with him around. I'm tired of carrying him, feeding him, and protecting him. It's time that bird found another friend to*

106

watch over him. And Rudy told Chip exactly what he thought.

"Well," Chip chirped, trying to hide his hurt, "I'm tired of picking your ticks. And I'm sick of looking out for you. You can just look out for yourself." And with that, Chip flew away.

Rudy enjoyed his first two days alone. But by the third day his hide began to itch from all the ticks that were tucked into his skin.

I'll live with them, he thought, as he rubbed against a tree. But Rudy didn't know that there was danger behind that tree.

"Shhh," one hunter warned another. "Rhinos are so nearsighted. He won't see us." And they raised their guns.

"Rudy, Rudy, guns behind you!" A high

voice chattered loudly. "TURN AROUND AND CHARGE!" Chip had been watching from a distance.

All humans know enough not to tangle with an angry rhino. So the hunters dropped their guns and ran. Maybe they are still running.

You can guess the end of this story. Rudy thanked Chip again and again. Now they laugh about their little argument. They tell anyone who will listen that good friends overlook each other's faults. After all, nobody is perfect.

Lilac's New Stripe

There was a time—long, long ago—when all skunks wore pure black coats. No skunk had a stripe. Lilac was the last of these black skunks. This is her story.

The woodland creatures loved Lilac, and she loved them. They all got along very well—except for Bluster the Bear. He liked to pester other creatures; sometimes he bullied them.

Lilac usually kept Bluster in line. When he threatened or bullied others, Lilac would spray him. Then he wouldn't bother anyone for a long, long time. And all the creatures would live in peace again.

This worked very well until Lilac made a mistake one night. As she sat beneath a bush to dig out its root for food, she heard soft grunts and snorts. They came closer and closer. Twigs snapped and branches broke. Then the bush above her began to sway and snap. *Bluster!* she thought. *He's after me!* Quickly she stood

up, took aim, and sprayed toward the noise.

But it wasn't Bluster. It was Dancie Deer. "Dancie, I'm so sorry," Lilac cried. "I should have looked first, but there wasn't time."

"It's not your fault," Dancie snuffled. "I should have spoken, but I didn't see you."

"Of course not," squeaked Dewey the Mouse. "How can you see a black animal in the dark?"

Lilac shuffled off to bed, very sad and a little embarrassed.

The next morning, Dewey scampered into her den. "Lilac, Lilac, wake up!" he squeaked. "I've got a great idea! Come outside with me."

Lilac rubbed her sleepy eyes and rolled out of her den. Just outside her door was

a huge can of white paint and a little brush.

"White shines in the dark," Dewey explained. "If we put this down your back, everyone will see it."

So Dewey painted a white stripe on Lilac. He started at her nose, then ran it over her head and down to the tip of her tail.

That day all the woodland creatures came to admire Lilac's new stripe. Even Bluster ambled by.

"Well," he muttered. "Nobody can miss you now."

And nobody could. In fact, the stripe worked so well that other woodlots soon heard about it. Before long, all black skunks wore beautiful white stripes. Now all woodland creatures recognize skunks, even on the blackest nights.

And that is why, to this day, skunks wear stripes and bears always respect skunks.

The Talking Tail

Shirley Squirrel stands with her bag of nuts and chatters at you. Do you know what she's saying? Most people don't

understand squirrel language. But Shirley talks with her tail too. If you try, you can understand her talking tail.

If she carries her tail straight back from herself, all is well. Shirley is friendly and thinks you are too.

If her tail waves up and down slowly, Shirley is a bit concerned. She's saying, "I don't know if you are really my friend."

If she jerks her tail up and down very quickly, Shirley is very upset. She's saying, "Stay away from me and my nuts."

If you move away from her, she'll probably feel better. She'll hold her tail flat against her back to say, "The danger has passed."

If she can't see you, she'll uncurl her tail

from her back. Then it will wave out again, because she knows all is well.

The next time you see a squirrel, watch to see what its tail is saying.

Wally's Distress

Sea creatures pass a wonderful old story from parents to children. It's called "Wally's Distress" and it goes like this:

118

Many years ago—long before anyone knew the difference between fishes, whales, dolphins, and dragons—there lived a whale named Wally. He swam the Great Sea and made his home in its eastern shallows.

One day, a very fierce storm blew above that sea. Because churning water usually carries rich food, Wally swam beneath that storm to eat. As he ate he swallowed one strange morsel that he had never eaten before.

There was no trash in the ocean at this time. Yet, that one strange morsel gave Wally many problems. His stomach felt awful. Then it tickled, then it ached, and then tied itself into wiggling knots.

For three days he couldn't eat or sleep. He thrashed around miserably and thought he would never be comfortable again.

So he called to the Creator for advice. Soon he found himself swimming easily—almost pushed, he often said—to the most shallow part of his home. Then his stomach knotted in such pain that he rose straight out of the water. He opened his mouth to cry, and the strange morsel popped right out onto the beach.

Wally realized then that he had swallowed a human. Yet the human was whole

and unharmed. He scrambled up the beach, and they both felt very much better.

Sea creatures tell "Wally's Distress" to show how the Creator cares for them. Humans tell the same story for the same reason. They call it "Jonah and the Whale."

Coats for the Yaks

Many years ago all yaks lived on farms with cattle and oxen, their close cousins. Very quiet by nature, the yaks soon tired of the loud noises.

"It's yakkity-yakkity-yak all day long," they said. "Let's find some peace and quiet." So they moved far up into the mountains away from the noise.

The yaks loved their new home. They had plenty of space. Swamp grass, herbs, and lichen—their favorite foods—grew everywhere. And it was quiet; most animals lived far down the mountains.

But there was one problem. The weather was very, very cold. And the yaks—like their cousins—had no coats.

So they asked the Creator to give them coats. "If this land is good for us," they said, "the Creator will help."

And he did. The Creator gave each yak a long, thick, hairy coat. He even put hair on each tail and a tassel at the end. Forever after yaks have lived warm and snug in their quiet mountain home.

Most animals have some kind of coat. But the coats made just for the yaks are special. They're called yackets.

What Are You?

"What are you?" the little monkey asked the zebra. "Are you a black horse with white stripes or a white horse with black stripes?"

"I don't know," the little zebra answered. "I never thought about that. Does that matter?"

"Of course it matters," said the little monkey who thought he knew everything. "Little things like that always matter. I'll come back in three days. By then you must tell me."

So the little zebra asked everyone he saw. But no one knew the answer.

Finally he went to the Creator and boldly asked, "Am I a black horse with

white stripes or a white horse with black stripes?"

"My dear little creature," the Creator began. And he talked to the zebra for a long, long time.

Three days later the monkey returned. "Well," he demanded, "what are you?"

"I'm a zebra," came the answer. "It

doesn't matter if I'm black with white stripes or white with black stripes. What matters is that I'm the best zebra I can be."

The know-it-all monkey didn't know what to say. But he never bothered the zebra again.